Giggle, Giggle, Quack

ARTIST'S NOTE

For this book I did brush drawings using Winsor & Newton lamp black watercolour on tracing paper. I then had the drawings photocopied onto one-ply Strathmore kid finish watercolour paper and applied watercolour washes to the black drawings. The advantage of this method is that I can get as many copies on the watercolour paper as I want, and I can experiment with the colour, choosing the finishes that I like the best.

SIMON & SCHUSTER

First published in Great Britain in 2003 by Simon & Schuster UK Ltd
Africa House, 64-78 Kingsway, London WC2B 6AH

Originally published in the USA in 2002 by Atheneum Books for Young Readers, an imprint of Simon & Schuster
Children's Publishing Division, New York

A CIP catalogue record for this book is available from the British Library upon request

Book design by Anahid Hamparian
The text of this book is set in 30-point Filosofia Bold

ISBN: 0 689 83723 2

Printed in Hong Kong

1 3 5 7 9 10 8 6 4 2

For Andrew
— D. C.

For Rosanne Lauer
— B. L.

Giggle, Giggle, Quack

by Doreen Cronin   pictures by Betsy Lewin

Simon & Schuster
London   New York   Sydney

Farmer Brown was going on holiday. He left his brother, Bob, in charge of the animals.

"I wrote everything down for you.
Just follow my instructions and
everything will be fine. But keep
an eye on Duck. He's trouble."

Farmer Brown thought he heard giggles and snickers as he drove away, but he couldn't be sure.

Bob gave Duck a good long stare
and went inside.
He read the first note:

Tuesday night
is pizza night
(not the frozen
kind!).
The hens prefer
anchovies.

Giggle, giggle, cluck.

Twenty-nine minutes later
there was hot pizza in the barn.

Bob checked on the animals
before he went to bed.
Everything was just fine.

Wednesday is bath day for the pigs.
Wash them with my favourite bubble bath and dry them off with my good towels.
Remember, they have very sensitive skin.

Giggle, giggle, oink.

Bob had all the pigs washed in no time.

Farmer Brown phoned home on
Wednesday night to check in.
"Did you feed the animals as
I wrote in the note?" he asked.

"Done," replied Bob, counting seven empty pizza boxes.

"Did you see my note about the pigs?"
"All taken care of," said Bob proudly.

"Are you keeping a very close eye on Duck?" he asked.

Bob gave Duck a good long stare. Duck was too busy sharpening his pencil to notice.

"Just keep him in the house," ordered Farmer Brown. "He's a bad influence on the cows."

Giggle, giggle, moo, giggle, oink, giggle, quack.

Thursday night is movie night. It's the cows' turn to pick.

Giggle, giggle, moo.

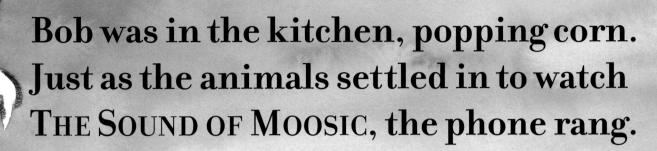

Bob was in the kitchen, popping corn.
Just as the animals settled in to watch
THE SOUND OF MOOSIC, the phone rang.

The only thing Farmer Brown heard on the other end was:

"Giggle, giggle, quack, giggle, moo, giggle, oink ..."

UH-OH.

"DUCK!"

screamed Farmer Brown.